Mariah Finds a Way

Reach Incorporated | Washington, DC

Shout Mouse Press

Reach Incorporated / Shout Mouse Press
Published by
Shout Mouse Press, Inc.
www.shoutmousepress.org

Copyright © 2014 Reach Education, Inc.
ISBN-13: 978-0692300824 (Shout Mouse Press, Inc.)
ISBN-10: 0692300821

For all those who were ever told,
"You can't..."

One day, Mariah overheard her mom and dad talking about their upcoming vacation. They were going to Jamaica for the week and were planning to close their family's fruit shop while they were gone. They didn't want just anybody in the store, and they didn't think they had anyone responsible enough to take care of it.

Mariah was heartbroken.

"Mom and Dad, let me run the store! I can do it."

Her mom paused. "I'm not sure if you can run the store by yourself," she said. She didn't say why, but of course Mariah knew. Mariah was blind. But so what? Didn't they tell her she could do anything?

Her dad saw Mariah getting upset. "Maybe we should give her a chance," he said. "She's been working in this store since she was little."

"*Crawk*, Give her a chance! *Crawk*, Give her a chance!" Blue, their pet parrot, blurted.

Her dad chuckled. "Honey, I think she can do it. Just give her a chance."

"Hmmmmm," said her mom. She did not look convinced.

Soon the day arrived when Mariah's parents were leaving. Mariah and her dad had tried to change her mom's mind, but it didn't work. The store would be closed.

Beep Beep!

"Honey, I think that's the cab. C'mon," Mariah's dad said. He picked up their bags and headed out the door.

"I'll walk y'all to the car," Mariah said disappointedly.

On his way there, Mariah's dad bent over like he was tying his shoe and left the keys to the fruit shop on the ground. He whistled and Blue flew over and scooped the keys into his mouth.

Mariah hugged her mother goodbye at the cab.
She hugged her dad, too.

"Don't forget to feed Blue his blueberries,"
he whispered in her ear.

Mariah walked back to the house, confused.
*Wait, what? Feed him his blueberries? How can I
feed him blueberries without getting into the store?*

At that moment, Blue perched on her shoulder and
dropped the keys to the fruit shop in her hand.

"*Crawk*, Blueberries!" he said.

Mariah gasped. "The keys!" She couldn't believe it.

The cab beeped as it pulled away. Mariah waved in the direction of her parents and
smiled wide.

Mariah did not waste any time. She walked right down the street to the store, hearing her neighbors talking and saying hello as she went by. She smelled the fresh air. She was so excited to run the store. This store had always been part of her family, so it meant a lot to her. She was determined to do a good job.

When Mariah arrived at the store, she created an inventory in her mind.

She walked around and touched all the fruit: the apples, the peaches, the mangos, the pears. When she couldn't figure out the fruit by touch, she took a bite.

Mariah taught herself to use the cash register and figured out where everything was by its size and shape and texture. She felt ready to go.

Just after nine o'clock, the bell on the door jingled as her first customer walked in. "Welcome!" she called out.

"I'm in a big hurry and I need lots of fruit," he said. "Can you help me with this list?" He handed over a piece of paper.

"This isn't going to help me very much," she said, pointing to her white cane. "But, if you read it to me, I'll be glad to help."

"Oh," he mumbled awkwardly. "I don't have time for that."

She heard the bell again. He had walked right out of the store.

Mariah sat in the silence of the empty store. She started to doubt herself. Could she really do this alone?

Mariah went outside and started to cry. Maybe her mother was right. She couldn't really see the amount of money that people handed her. And she could only rely on touch, smell, hearing, and taste to get around the store. What if she messed up? She hadn't worried about these things before, but now she had lost confidence. How did that happen so quickly?

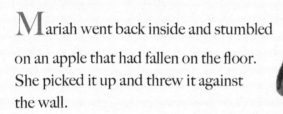

Mariah went back inside and stumbled on an apple that had fallen on the floor. She picked it up and threw it against the wall.

Blue said, "*Crawk*, Fifty-four cents!"
Mariah was amazed. "You know the prices?!"
"Of course I do," he said. "I've been working in this store for twenty years, but no one ever asked me."
Suddenly Mariah felt a burst of hope. "Do you want to help me?"
"Of course, that's all I've ever wanted to do!" Blue said.

Now she had a plan.

Mariah was feeling better when she got home that night. She made herself some dinner and checked her voicemails. The first message started and she recognized her father's voice.

"Hey Mariah, just wanted to let you know we got here safe. Don't forget to feed Blue his blueberries. I believe in you."

When she heard her dad's code words, she was happy. This was a big responsibility. She didn't want to let her dad down.

As she went to bed that night, Mariah thought to herself, *With Blue's help and Dad's support, I'm going to show Mom I can do this.*

The next day Mariah got out of bed determined. She went to the shop and woke up Blue. She fed him his favorite fruit: blueberries.

Blue did a backflip and whistled his blueberry song.

Crawk!
This is my blueberry song.
Crawk!
I eat them berries all day long.
Crawk!
I love the way they taste.
Crawk!
And the juice runs down my face.

Crawk!
Man, I love the way they taste.
More than fat kids love their cake...

Suddenly, Blue got interrupted when the bell went jingle jangle.

He said, "*Crawk*, Someone's at the door!"

Mariah headed to the cash register to get ready for her first sale.

The customer brought a bag full of fruit to the counter. Mariah felt the fruit and told Blue what she had. Blue called out the price and did the calculations. Mariah made the sale, and the customer left with a "Thank you!"

Mariah stuck her hand in the air and said, "Our first sale! High fly!"

Blue flew right into her hand. It was their own special celebration.

Next an old person walked into the store. He had a belly like Santa Claus with a big white beard, but he was wearing regular clothes. He wore big boots, and his coat had lots of pockets. He had a scar on his face, too. As he walked around the store, Mariah smelled the scent of freshly baked bread.

"I have to go to the little birdie's room," Blue said quietly.
"Okay," she said, "but hurry back."

In the meantime, the man had noticed Mariah's white cane leaning against the counter. He got a creepy smile on his face and began stuffing fruit in all his pockets. As he walked up to the counter, he had fruit in every pocket and three watermelons stuffed under his shirt.

The man placed an apple on the counter. Mariah remembered that an apple cost fifty-four cents and told him the price. He gave her a dollar and said in a voice that reminded her of Alvin and the Chipmunks, "Keep the change." He walked out of the store just as Blue returned.

"Hey," Mariah said with a smile, "that man just gave me our first tip!"

But Mariah's excitement didn't last long.

A little boy who had been in the store picking up oranges for his mother walked up to the counter. He said, "Didn't you see that man just stole from you?"

"What?" Mariah said. "Actually, no, I can't see. What happened?" she asked.

"He had a bunch of fruit in his pockets and some watermelons under his shirt," the little boy said quietly.

Blue squawked, "*Crawk*, We've been robbed!"

Mariah wanted to cry, but she tried to stay tough because she was in charge.

"I'm not going to let that guy get to me," she said. She turned to Blue. "You and Dad believe in me, so I can't let you down."

Mariah wiped away the couple of tears that slipped down her cheek and finished the sale with the little boy.

"*Crawk*, Seventy-five cents for the oranges!" Blue said.

"Thank you for telling me about the guy who robbed us," Mariah said. "If he ever comes back, I'll be ready."

Mariah got home that night just as the phone was ringing. She picked up and it was her mom on the line.

"How is everything going?" her mom asked. "I overheard you and your dad talk about Blue's blueberries. I should have left you some at the house! So sorry. Is he going crazy without them?"
"Umm, he's fine," Mariah said, hoping her mother wouldn't ask anything more.
"*Crawk*, Blueberries!" Blue said.
"Shhhhhh!" said Mariah.
"Well, okay," her mother said. "We'll be home in a few days and we can give him plenty then."

When Mariah hung up her heart was racing, but she had an idea.

"Blue, we need a code word, like Dad and I have. That way, if someone tries to rob us again, we can use it. How about this: If you hear me say "star fruit," that means I think we're getting robbed. Fly to the police and bring them back so we can catch the thief!"

"*Crawk*, Star fruit!" Blue said.

A couple days passed, and Mariah and Blue did well with only a few mistakes.

On the first day, a customer came in and bought a cantaloupe, but Mariah gave him the wrong change because she couldn't read the bills.

After that, she taught Blue to call out the money in funny ways:
"*Crawk*, That's a fiver! *Crawk*, Twenty smackers!"

It made the customers laugh. Soon the word spread about the blind girl and her parrot running the store, and Mariah was selling more and more fruit every day.

She felt proud of herself, and she couldn't wait for her parents to see what a great job she had done.

The day Mariah's parents were supposed to come home, Mariah heard the jingle of the store's bell and said her usual hello to the customer who walked in.

"Hello!" a high-pitched man's voice said.

Mariah thought to herself, *I remember that voice from somewhere.* She didn't want to jump to conclusions, so she asked him a question.

"How is your day going, sir?"

"I'm fine. Just picking up some fruit for a pie I'm making."

Mariah sensed the man walking around the store, leaving traces of a bakery smell. She was confident that it was the same guy who stole from her before. She started to follow him around, listening to his footsteps. She felt the shelves as she passed by and noticed that fruit was missing.

"Sir, do you want to try some of our new STAR FRUITS?" Mariah said, loud enough for Blue to hear.

The man looked up and saw Blue flying out of the store.

This is a perfect opportunity to rob them again, he thought.

"Sure, I'll try some as I pay for this apple."

Mariah went to the counter and began chopping the star fruit. She took her time, chopping very very slowly. She wanted to make sure that the man stayed long enough for the police to arrive. She could hear him shifting back and forth on his feet. Finally she handed the man a cup full of the sample.

"Thanks, but I don't like this fruit very much," he said quickly. "I'm in a rush. I have a pie that's baking right now and needs these apples to make it complete."

Mariah didn't know what to do, but she took the money from the man anyway. She was worried that he was about to get away.

"Wait a second!" she called out. She picked up a watermelon as he walked toward the door. "Thanks for the tip," she said, and she threw the watermelon at him with all her might.

Shocked, the man caught the watermelon, but another one fell from beneath his shirt, and he fell to the ground like a bowling pin.

As the man began to climb to his feet, Blue swooped in and the police came rushing in the door. They told the man to put his hands in the air, and all of the fruit began to fall out of his pockets.

"*Crawk*, That's the robber! *Crawk*, Freeze!"

As more of the fruit fell out of his shirt, the police put the man in handcuffs.

Just then, Mariah's parents pulled up to the fruit store. The police car was filling the shop with blue and red lights.

"Are you okay, Mariah? What happened? What are you doing here? We went home and you weren't there!" Mariah's mom asked worriedly.

"Honey, this is my fault," said her dad. "I thought she could do it..."

"I did do it," Mariah said confidently. "We got robbed, but I caught the robber."

Her mother looked from Mariah to the policeman in shock.

"She's right," the cop said. "We've been chasing this guy for months. He's been robbing food stores all over the city. Your daughter is the only one who's caught him. She's a real hero, and she'll get a big reward."

Mariah felt her face light up.

"It looks like you were right," Mariah's mom said to her dad.

She turned to Mariah. "And you were right, too. I'm sorry. I should've believed in you all along."

...h got a big
...own. It was
...robber.

...n as the town

...and said, "I'm
so proud of you...

Then she turned to Mariah's dad
with a smirk on her face and said,
"Maybe we should go on vacation
more often."

Acknowledgments

In July 2014, twelve students embarked on an exciting journey. Tasked with the challenge of creating original children's books that reflected the diversity and reality of their world, these young people brainstormed ideas, generated potential plots, wrote, revised, and provided critiques. In the end, they created four amazing books, showing again what teenagers can do when their potential is unleashed with purpose. Our twelve authors have our immense gratitude and respect: Kyare, Za'Metria, Litzi, Makayla, Darrin, Marc, Darne'sha, Zorita, Karta, Ashley, Rico, and Daequan.

These books are a joint project between Reach Incorporated and Shout Mouse Press, and we are grateful for the leadership provided by members of both teams. From Reach, Leigh Creighton and Jeremiah Headen acted as all-important story scribes, working closely with authors to capture and develop their ideas. We simply wouldn't have been able to do it without our incredible Summer Program Director, Jusna Perrin.

From the Shout Mouse Press team, we thank Alison Klein and Annie Rosenthal for their guidance as story scribes, and Lucia Liu and Mira Ko for their beautiful illustrations. Kathy Crutcher served as story coach and series editor. We are grateful for the time and talents of these writers and artists!

Most of all, we thank those of you who have purchased the books. It is your support that allows us to support teen authors in engaging young readers. We hope the smiles created as you read match those expressed as we wrote.

-- Mark Hecker
Reach Incorporated, Founder and Executive Director

About the Authors

Marc Gaskins is sixteen years old and is from Washington, DC. This is his second children's book. He is also a co-author of *The Airplane Effect*. Marc enjoys playing sports, cooking, and spending time with family and friends. As a junior this year Marc will be attending Ballou Senior High School.

Darrin Gladman was born in Washington, DC, and is in the tenth grade at Eastern Senior High School. He will graduate in 2017. Darrin is a very artistic and creative person who loves his family. He plans on being a graphic designer or doing cyber security as his future career.

About the Authors

Makayla Sutton lives in Washington, DC, and she is in tenth grade. Makayla likes to hang out, go to parties, and have fun. But if not doing those things, she mostly has school on her mind. She is very helpful and loves working with kids and encouraging people.

About the Illustrator

Mira Ko is an illustrator residing in Richmond, VA. She is currently pursuing a BFA in Communication Arts with a minor in Painting and Printmaking at Virginia Commonwealth University. Her passion is for illustrating narratives, whether children's books, adult literature, magazine publications, or animation scripts. Her previous illustration credits include *The Gloomy Light* and *The Airplane Effect*. See more of her work at www.behance.com/mirako.

About Reach Incorporated

Reach Incorporated develops confident grade-level readers and capable leaders by training teens to teach younger students, creating academic benefit for all involved.

Founded in 2009, Reach recruits high school students to be elementary school reading tutors. Elementary school students average 1.5 grade levels of reading growth per year of participation. This growth – equal to that created by highly effective teachers – is created by high school students who average more than two grade levels of growth per year of program participation.

As skilled reading tutors, our teens noticed that the books they read with their students did not reflect their reality. At Reach, we trust teens with real responsibility for things that matter to them. So, when confronted with this challenge, we did what seemed most appropriate: we had our teens write new books. Through fanciful stories with diverse characters, our books invite young readers to explore the world through words.

By purchasing our books, you support student-led, community-driven efforts to improve educational outcomes in the District of Columbia.

Learn more about all our books at www.reachincorporated.org/books.

About Shout Mouse Press

Shout Mouse Press is a publishing house for unheard voices.

- We promote diversity in literature by empowering under-represented communities worldwide to develop and write their stories, and then we professionally publish them for a broad audience.
- We create tangible, marketable products for the nonprofits and communities we serve in order to amplify, diversify, and innovate their outreach and fundraising.

The founding of Shout Mouse Press was inspired by a collaboration with Reach Incorporated during the summer of 2013 when we helped their teen tutors produce their first set of original children's books. We witnessed the way those books expanded the horizons of possibility for both their authors and readers alike, and that emboldened us to bring the power of publication to more communities whose voices need to be heard. We now partner with nonprofit organizations serving communities in need and design book projects that help further their missions. Shout Mouse authors have produced original children's books, memoir collections, and novels-in-stories. Learn more at ShoutMousePress.org.

CPSIA information can be obtained
at www.ICGtesting.com
Printed in the USA
BVOW05s1033240117

474271BV00004B/7/P